OTTO
Has a Birthday Party

Todd PARR

Megan Tingley Books

LITTLE, BROWN AND COMPANY

New York ☞ An AOL Time Warner Company

To Tammy. You amaze and inspire me.
I love you very much—Todd

Also by Todd Parr

The Best Friends Book
Big & Little
Black & White
The Daddy Book
Do's and Don'ts
The Family Book
The Feel Good Book
The Feelings Book
Funny Faces
Going Places
It's Okay to Be Different
The Mommy Book
My Really Cool Baby Book
The Okay Book
Things That Make You Feel Good / Things That Make You Feel Bad
This Is My Hair
Underwear Do's and Don'ts
Zoo Do's and Don'ts

First Edition

Library of Congress Cataloging-in-Publication Data

Parr, Todd.
   Otto has a birthday party / Todd Parr.—1st ed.
     p. cm.
   Summary: There is a problem with the cake Otto the dog makes for his birthday party, but he and his friends have a good time anyway.
   ISBN 0-316-73907-3
     [1. Birthdays—Fiction. 2. Cake—Fiction. 3. Parties—Fiction. 4. Dogs — Fiction] I. Title.
PZ7.P2447 Ov 2004
[E]—dc21   2003040268

10 9 8 7 6 5 4 3 2 1

TWP

Printed in Singapore

Today is Otto's birthday, and he is going to make his cake all by himself.

Otto puts in a cup of flour, two shoes, three bones, some pepperoni, a cootie bug, and a hot dog.

He spreads mud all over
the top for frosting.
Then he puts the cake in
the oven.

One by one all of his friends
show up to the party...
a polka-dot dog,

a big dog and a little dog,

a wiener dog,

and even Cool Kitty the cat.

They play all of their favorite games, like Pin the Tail on the Cat.

Then Otto opens his presents. The first present is underwear, but it is too small.

"Sorry, Otto!"

The second is a sweater,
but it is too big.

"Sorry, Otto!"

The third is a brand-new
tennis ball that is just right.

"Yay, Otto."

Soon it is time for cake. But when Otto opens the oven door, the cake explodes! It makes a big mess and it is pretty stinky.

"Oh, no!" says Otto. "Everybody is waiting for cake. What am I going to do now?"

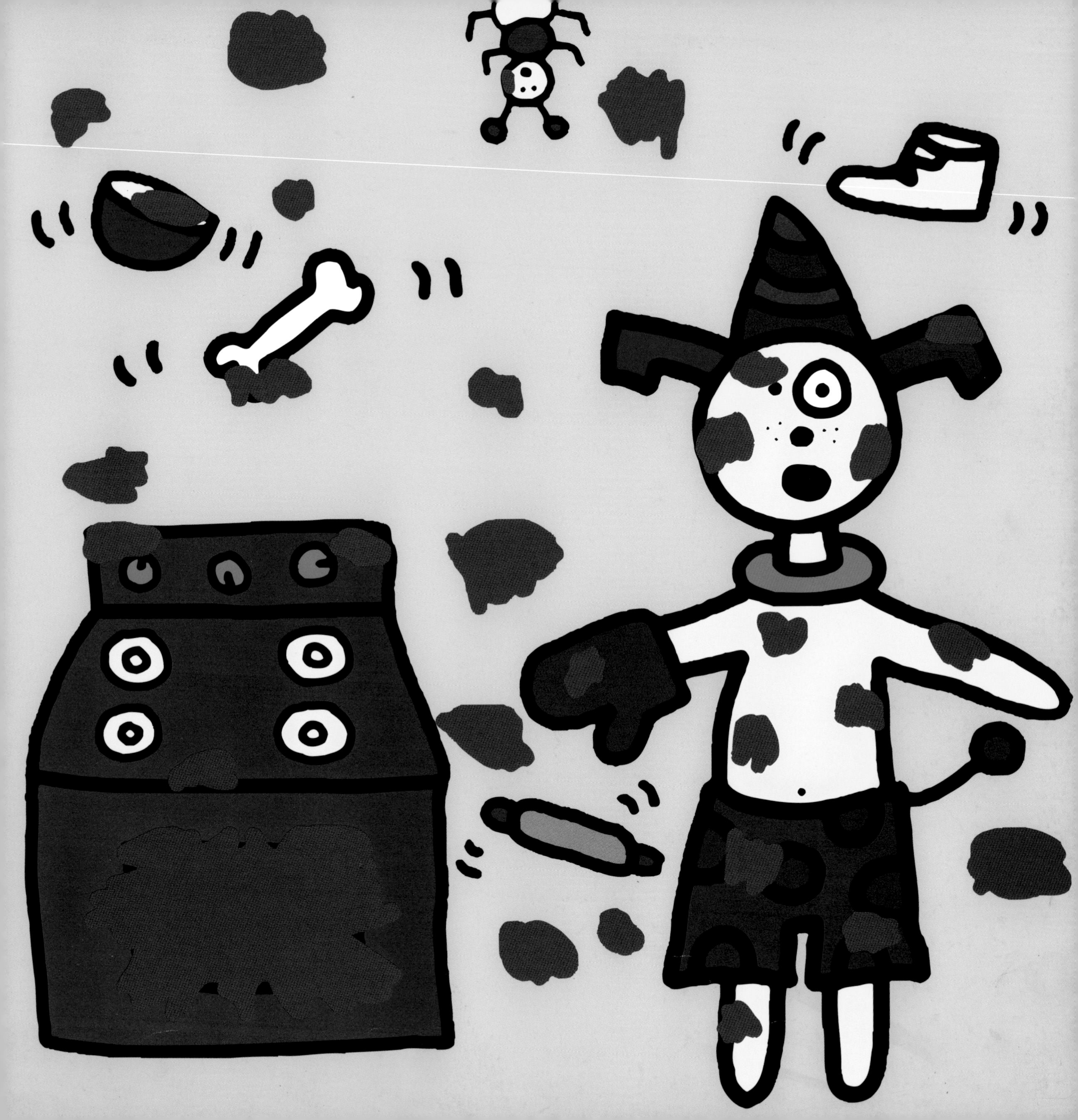

"Don't worry, Otto," say his friends. "Look out the window."

"Honk! Honk!" It's the ice-cream truck with a special delivery!

Everybody says it is the
best birthday party ever.

Have fun on your Birthday, but don't put a cootie bug or a shoe in your cake!

Love, ♥

OTTO and TODD